Anonymous

Memorial Sketch of Dr. William Frederick Poole, MDCCCXXI

Anonymous

Memorial Sketch of Dr. William Frederick Poole, MDCCCXXI

ISBN/EAN: 9783337097080

Printed in Europe, USA, Canada, Australia, Japan

Cover: Foto ©Raphael Reischuk / pixelio.de

More available books at **www.hansebooks.com**

Memorial Sketch

of

Dr. William Frederick Poole

mdccccxxi

Chicago: mdcccxcv

DR. WILLIAM FREDERICK POOLE was born in Salem, Massachusetts, on the 24th day of December, 1821. He was a lineal descendant, in the eighth generation, from John Poole, an English emigrant, who settled in Cambridge, Massachusetts, then known as Newtown, in 1632. Dr. Poole attended the common schools in Salem until twelve years of age, and thus acquired a fair knowledge of English branches, and had also, by study at home outside of his work in school, acquired a limited knowledge of the Latin grammar and higher mathematics. His plan of securing a college education at first seemed impracticable, from financial difficulties, but at the age of eighteen years, the way seemed

seemed clear, and he entered the academy at Leicester.   He remained at this academy for three years, during a part of which time he was one of the teachers, and in 1842, being sufficiently prepared, he entered the freshman class at Yale College.   He was, however, disappointed in his arrangements in regard to his college expenses, and at the end of his freshman year, left college and engaged in teaching, which pursuit he followed for three years, after which he returned to college and entered the class of 1849, as a sophomore, and was duly graduated, with high honors.   Among his classmates were President Timothy Dwight, of Yale College, and President Franklin Fisk, of Chicago Theological Seminary, with whom he maintained a life-long friendship.   Near the close of his sophomore year, he was chosen for the position of assistant librarian of

rian of the Society of Brothers of Unity, connected with which Society was a library of about ten thousand volumes. A considerable part of this library consisted of bound volumes, and, in many cases, of complete sets of the leading foreign quarterlies and magazines, and of the best American periodicals. At this time it was customary, in the college, for the topics for essays and other literary work to be announced from time to time in the college chapel, and Dr. Poole, in answer to an urgent demand for such information, presently commenced to post in the library, in connection with each of the topics thus announced, a list of the books in the library relating to such topics, and also a list of the articles in the various reviews and magazines which would be useful in the preparation of essays upon the topics announced. This proved to be of such

such value to the students, that
he decided to compile an index of
the contents of all the periodicals
in the library—a work which had
not been before attempted, and
which index was published during
his junior year, making a modest
octavo volume of 154 pages.　A
second edition was soon called for,
and as the work seemed to have
met a popular demand, he decided
to enlarge it, and during his senior
year and a part of the year following his graduation from college,
he prepared a new edition of the
index, embracing a large number
of periodicals not included in the
previous edition, making a volume
of something over five hundred
pages, which was published in
1853. Periodical literature to that
time had been much less volumi-
nous than at present, and was
also largely of a high character—
the most eminent literary and
scientific men of the old world
being,

being, as a rule, contributors to the well-known quarterlies of the period. The modest volumes, to which allusion has been made, demonstrated the need of a wider and more comprehensive work, and the result was, in later years, the volume known, as had been the preceding editions, as "Poole's Index to Periodical Literature," which made its name a household word in every library, as well as in the home of a great part of the men of letters of the whole civilized world.

THE present age has been one of remarkable progress, especially in every department of scientific research, and the method by which investigators make known to the world the progress of their work, by reason of this fact, has changed. Instead of spending many years, as formerly, in the preparation of a carefully elaborated volume, showing the

ing the results of years of research, the investigator now feels
apprehensive lest some co-worker
in the same field may anticipate
his discoveries, and, therefore, so
soon as he has material sufficient
for a good magazine article, it is
usually published in this method,
and when a sufficient number of
such contributions have been
made, the author collects them
and publishes a volume. Periodical literature, too, has enormously
increased in volume, and the valuable periodicals are today more
than one thousand in number.
For the reason just indicated the
freshest results of research in almost every department of human
knowledge are found in the pages
of the various periodicals, and,
inasmuch as no person has time
or opportunity to read all of these
periodicals, an index of their contents, which shall render them
available to the student in any
field

field of work, is indispensable, and Dr. Poole's early and almost boyish training in this work seemed to indicate him as the person especially fitted for carrying it forward. The result was the publication, in 1882, of the "Index to Periodical Literature," a royal octavo of fourteen hundred and sixty-nine pages, which represented the work of all his spare moments for many years. In this work he was largely assisted by Mr. William I. Fletcher, Librarian of Amherst College, who was associate editor of the work, and several librarians of the great English and American libraries were also called upon to assist in the work and to index several of the periodicals. Dr. Poole, however, had the final supervision of everything connected with this great work, and himself examined and corrected the proof sheets of every page of the Index. Five years

years after the publication of the first edition, a supplement was issued, bringing the work down to 1888, and a second supplement, largely the work of Mr. Fletcher, appeared in 1893.

DR. POOLE'S work in the library of the College Society, which has already been referred to, and the publication of the two editions of the Index, had made him well and favorably known in connection with library work, so that, soon after his graduation in 1851, he was chosen assistant Librarian of the Boston Athenaeum, and the following year was appointed Librarian of the Boston Mercantile Library, which position he held for four years. During his incumbency of this position, he prepared a catalogue of the library, upon a plan of his own, which was largely followed in other libraries, and is known as the "Dictionary Catalogue."

logue." In this catalogue, the author's name, title of the book, and the subjects, were arranged alphabetically, each entry occupying but a single line. The Mercantile Library at this time contained about sixteen thousand volumes. In 1856, he resigned the position of Librarian of the Mercantile Library to accept a like position in the Library of the Boston Athenaeum, where he remained for thirteen years, until January, 1869. Dr. Poole always referred to this period of his life as being especially filled with delightful memories. He was brought in contact with the most cultivated literary society of America. The men who were the principal contributors to the "Atlantic Monthly," in its early days, and to the "North American Review" of that period, among whom were Longfellow, Emerson, Lowell, Holmes, Ticknor, Charles Francis

Francis Adams and Parkman, as well as many of the younger writers, as Henry James, T. B. Aldrich, W. D. Howells and others, were his almost daily associates. The principal writers for the periodical literature of this day frequented the library of the Boston Athenaeum, and Dr. Poole always made special effort to procure for the library everything which would be useful to them in their literary work, and, by meeting them in constant friendly and literary intercourse, established personal relations and friendships with all the people who made illustrious this particular period of American literature, friendships which lasted during the lives of all these most interesting people.

THE first example of what is known as the "Dictionary Catalogue," carried out in a comprehensive method, was Dr. Poole's

Poole's catalogue, before referred to, of the Boston Mercantile Library. Before that time books had been usually catalogued under various systems of classification, the volumes being grouped from their general subjects, as historical, theological, medical, literary, etc. No two persons would, of course, ever agree in the systems of classification, so that no catalogue made upon that plan would be satisfactory to all classes of readers. The method originated by Dr. Poole was at once much more simple, as well as more satisfactory. The books were catalogued alphabetically, as to the name of the author, title of book, and the subject or subjects treated in the volumes, and this method, modified and enlarged as subsequent experience dictated, including careful systems of cross-references, is now in universal use, and is the only method by which the

the riches of a great library can be made immediately available to students, as not only all the volumes on a special subject, but all portions of volumes wherein the same subject is discussed, appear in the catalogue under the subject heading.

AFTER leaving the position of librarian of the Boston Athenaeum, Dr. Poole worked for several years as an expert in the formation and building up of libraries in various parts of the country. His experience in library work made him an invaluable adviser in the formation of city or college libraries. He could make up a list of books which would be most desirable and most called for in a library of a few thousand volumes, thus giving to the library the benefit of his wide experience and saving it from the mistakes often made in the purchase of books for a library

library by those unfamiliar with
the work. Among the libraries,
in regard to which he was con-
sulted in this way, was that of
Cincinnati, and a considerable
sum of money having become
available for the city library, he
accepted there the position of
Librarian, organized the library
to a high standard of efficiency,
and continued in this position
until he was called to a similar
work in Chicago, soon after the
great fire. His work in Cincinnati occupied five years, and his
services are looked upon by the
people of that city, in the organizing and planning of the work
of the library along lines which
have since been followed, as permanent and invaluable. Soon
after the great fire in Chicago, an
ordinance was adopted, in con-
formity with the State Law, pro-
viding a tax levy for each year
for the purpose of a public library,
and

and Dr. Poole was selected as the man most eminently qualified for the work of organizing this library. He held this position for about thirteen years, and until the Chicago Public Library had grown from nothing to a collection of over one hundred and fifty thousand volumes. This library was popular in its character, it being one of Dr. Poole's most steadfast opinions that, while all immoral books should be excluded, nearly everything outside of this line should be provided to meet the public demand. He used to say that it was much better for a person to read slush and the most foolish novels rather than not to read at all, that the reading of any book induced the taste for farther reading, and that the people who commenced by reading the most worthless books in the library would gradually have their taste formed for higher work,

work, and would become readers of works of positive value.

IN 1887, Dr. Poole resigned the position of Librarian of the Chicago Public Library to accept the same position in the Newberry Library—the fund donated for the establishment of this library by Walter L. Newberry having then become available. It had been decided to make this library one of reference simply, in other words, a library for scholars and people desiring to make careful researches in standard works for their own mental training, or for purposes of literary work. This was a task much more to his taste than anything which had come to him in his previous experience, inasmuch as it would ultimately bring him in contact largely with educators and literary workers. This position he held until the time of his death, in March, 1894, at which time the library

library had on its shelves about one hundred thousand volumes of carefully selected works of value and importance to students and workers in nearly every field of intellectual effort.

ANY memoir of the life and work of Dr. Poole would be most inadequate which did not make full mention of his own literary work. He was descended from a line of Puritan ancestors, and still preserved in his own character the most valuable traits of those antique heroes of our commonwealth. The narrowness of some of the earlier Puritans had passed away in the process of time, leaving permanent, however, the high regard for all that was best in the work of the Church and State. One of the publications which first brought the literary work of Dr. Poole prominently before the public was his essay, afterwards enlarged, in regard

regard to the connection of Dr.
Cotton Mather with the prosecution of supposed witches in Salem,
Massachusetts. Salem being Dr.
Poole's birth place, he made himself thoroughly familiar with
everything available regarding
its early history. Some writer,
upon insufficient examination, had
made the statement that Dr.
Mather originated the prosecution
of various people for witchcraft,
such prosecutions being in many
cases followed by the death of
the alleged criminal. This dic-
tum, not having been questioned,
had passed into common belief,
and various historical writers
upon the early period of New
England had stated this as an
unquestioned fact. Dr. Poole's
examination of the history of
Salem satisfied him that these
statements were absolutely erro-
neous, and his papers upon the
subject have entirely reversed the
previous

previous findings of local history upon this point. Another of the valuable contributions to American History was made by Dr. Poole, while Librarian at Cincinnati, in a paper showing the real origin of the famous ordinance of 1787, by which slavery was finally excluded from the northwestern territory. After the agitation of the slavery question had become one of the leading features in American politics, great credit had been given to certain members of congress for the introduction and passage of this famous ordinance, and their foresight, sagacity and anti-slavery proclivities were most highly commended by anti-slavery supporters and writers. Dr. Poole's researches made clear the fact that the ordinance of 1787, so far as its special promoters and the members of congress were concerned, had no underlying moral purpose, but was

was purely a matter of business.
Vast tracts of land in Ohio had
been taken up, under the provi-
sions of a law passed soon after
the revolutionary war, allowing
the holders of the badly depre-
ciated government currency and
securities to purchase land there-
with. The owners of this land
were anxious to induce settlers to
go upon it, and as the class of
settlers they were endeavoring to
influence were almost entirely
from New England, and were
opponents of slavery, the owners
of the land felt that, could it be
absolutely determined that the
great Northwest would be free
from slavery, it would be much
less difficult to induce colonies
from New England to purchase
land. The moral and humane
side of this great ordinance is,
therefore, to be credited solely to
the people of New England, the
expected settlers of the great
Northwest,

Northwest, whose views on the question of slavery had thus early taken form, and in deference to which views the famous law was enacted.

DR. POOLE found, in Marietta, Ohio, the diary of Dr. Manasseh Cutler, who had been the agent of the New England land companies, and had spent a winter in Washington to secure the passage of the ordinance of 1787, in which diary the object of such ordinance as aiding in the sale of land, and the settlement of the western country, is constantly adverted to. Lobbying in those days would seem, from the extracts given by Dr. Poole from this diary, to be a much less expensive process than at the present time, the good Dr. Cutler's method being simply to invite, from time to time, three or four members of congress to a dinner at his boarding house, where the matter

matter would be discussed over
a somewhat more elaborate menu
than the prevailing simplicity of
diet in Washington. Another interesting feature was brought out
in this journal, being the fact that
many of the most earnest supporters of the ordinance of 1787
were from the slave - holding
states, but at that time the slave-
holding states were the most
wealthy part of the nation, and
the representatives of those
states, looking upon the national
indebtedness as enormous and as
a menace to the future growth of
the nation, were especially anxious
to forward any measure for the
reduction of the public debt, and
the prospect of a large portion
of the government indebtedness
being used in the purchase of
land was the argument which, to
the southern members of congress, had special weight.

The

THE Puritan proclivities of Dr. Poole, to which allusion has already been made, resulted in his literary work being largely confined to the discussion of historical problems connected with the settlement of New England. He wrote many admirable reviews of historical works, and the last article from his pen, published in the "Dial" shortly before his death, was a scathing review of a historical work by Charles Francis Adams, in which Dr. Poole hotly resented certain remarks of Mr. Adams, criticising the work, methods and character of the Puritan Fathers. A careful and accurate bibliography of the contributions of Dr. Poole to various magazines and critical journals has been prepared by his intimate friend, Mr. D. L. Shorey, and is annexed to this memoir.

Outside

OUTSIDE the work of Dr.
Poole in historical matters
and in criticisms of historical
work, he wrote numerous and
valuable papers upon the subject
of library management and library construction. His position
in regard to library buildings for
a time aroused much antagonism,
although ultimately the correct-
ness of his views has been gener-
ally recognized, and the newer
library buildings are largely
modeled upon some adaptation of
his ideas. The early method of
a great library building was to
have the interior something like
the nave of a great church, with
the books arranged about the
wall and reached by staircases.
Dr. Poole attacked this method
upon the ground that it was a
great waste of room ; that it was
extremely inconvenient to reach
the books ; and that the books in
the upper part of the room were
injured

injured by the excessive heat.
The building occupied by the
Newberry Library is the best ex-
emplification of Dr. Poole's ideas
of library construction. This
building was constructed upon
Dr. Poole's plans, by the original
trustees, under the will of Mr.
Newberry. Heretofore the usual
method had been to bring the
books from all parts of the library
to one great and general reading
room. His idea was to so classify
the books as to separate them
into a few great departments,
each of which would have its own
room, and to have tables for the
use of readers in each room, and
an attendant, who would in time
become familiar with all the books
in that special department, and
would thus be able to serve the
readers with promptness, to assist
them in the selection of books,
and, on the part of the readers, to
make the room more quiet and
suitable

suitable for work than were they obliged to do this work in a large room used by all the readers in the library.

DR. POOLE'S long experience in the chosen work of his life had given him an almost unequalled familiarity with books and enabled him to point out to any person desiring to familiarize himself with any special subject the books best adapted for his use. He was the Nestor of American Librarians, and aided all the younger members in the work which he had done so much to raise to the rank of one of the learned professions, and to whom he was always most courteous, friendly and helpful. All the results of his vast experience were placed at their service, and his uniform courtesy and kindness made him unnumbered friends among the members of his own profession. In all parts of the country

country, where public libraries have been organized, the value of his services can be seen and appreciated, although the two libraries, which will be for him his most enduring monuments, are the two in our own city, where he spent the last nineteen years of a long, honorable and useful life.

IN recognition of these services, the Board of Trustees of the Newberry Library direct that this brief outline of his invaluable work in the cause of education and literature, be spread in full upon the minutes, and that a copy of the same be sent to his family.

Bibliography

WILLIAM FREDERICK POOLE.

Dictionaries in the Boston Libraries.
Springfield, 1856. 8vo. 8 pp.

Websterian Orthography; a Reply to Dr.
Noah Webster's Calumniators. Boston,
1857. 8vo. 23 pp.

The Orthographical Hobgoblin. Springfield, 1859. 8vo. 14 pp.

The Popham Colony; a Discussion of its
Historical Claims, with a Bibliography
of the Subject. Boston, 1866. 8vo.
72 pp.

The Wonder-Working Providence of
Sion's Saviour in New England. Lon-
don, 1654, by Edward Johnson, reprinted,
with an Historical Introduction by W.
F. Poole (154 pp.), and an Index (23 pp.)
Andover, 1867. 4to. 419 pp.

The Popham Colony. North American
Review, October, 1868. Vol. 107, pp.
663-674.

The Mather Papers; Cotton Mather and
Salem Witchcraft. Boston Daily Ad-
vertiser, Oct. 28, 1868.

The Same, Privately Printed, Boston, 1868.
12mo. 23 pp.

Anne

Anne Bradstreet, the Early New England
    Poetess.   North   American   Review.
    1868.   Vol. 106, pp. 330-334.
Cotton Mather   and   Salem Witchcraft.
    North American Review, April, 1869.
    Vol. 108, pp. 337-397.
The Same, Privately Printed.   Boston,
    1869.   63 pp.
Cotton   Mather   and   Witchcraft;   two
    Notices of Mr. Upham, his Reply.
    Privately Printed, Boston, 1870. 12mo.
    30 pp.   (From Watchman and Reflector,
    Boston, May 5, 1870, and Christian Era,
    Boston, April 23, 1870.)
The Witchcraft Delusion of 1692, by Gov.
    Thomas Hutchinson, from an unpub-
    lished MS.; with notes by Wm. F.
    Poole.   New England Historical and
    Genealogical Register, Oct., 1870.   Vol.
    24, pp. 381-414.
The Same, Privately Printed, Boston,
    1870.   4to.   43 pp.
Anti-Slavery Opinions before the year 1800.
    Cincinnati, 1872.   8vo.   102 pp.
The Tyler Davidson Fountain.   Cincin-
    nati, 1872.   8vo.   118 pp.
The Same, Illustrated.   Cincinnati, 1872.
    Roy. 4to.
The Owl, a Literary Monthly.   Chicago.
    1874-75.   4to.
                                      The

The Ordinance of 1787, and Dr. Manasseh
Cutler, as an Agent in its Formation.
North American Review for April, 1876.
Vol. 122, pp. 229-265.
The Same, Privately Printed. Cambridge,
1876. 8vo. 38 pp.
Witchcraft in Boston. In Winsor's Mem-
orial History of Boston, 1881. Vol. 2,
pp. 131-172.
The West; from the Treaty of Peace with
France, 1763, to the Treaty of Peace
with England, 1783. In Winsor's Nar-
rative and Critical History of America.
Vol. 6, pp. 685-743.
The Early Northwest ; The President's
Address, Dec. 26, 1888. Papers of the
American Historical Association, Vol. 3,
pp. 275-300.
The Same, Privately Printed, New York,
1889. 8vo. 26 pp.
Roosevelt's The Winning of the West.
Atlantic Monthly, Nov. 1889. Vol. 44,
pp. 693-700.
The Ordinance of 1787 ; a Reply. The In-
lander (Ann Arbor), Jan., 1892, pp.
169-181.
The Same, Privately Printed, Ann Arbor,
1892. 15 pp.
Columbus and the Finding of the New
World. Northwestern Christian Advo-
cate, Oct. 19, 1892.
The

The Same, Privately Printed, Chicago, 1892. 12mo.

The Dial, Chicago:

Vol. I, 1881-82. Hildreth's History of the United States, p. 1; Dexter's History of Congregationalism, p. 69; Winsor's Memorial History of Boston, p. 152; Father Hennepin, p. 253.

Vol. II, 1881-82. Lodge's History of the English Colonies in America, p. 32; The Yorktown Campaign, 1781, p. 111; Lossing's Popular Cyclopedia of United States History, p. 209; General Arthur St. Clair, pp. 227 251.

Vol. III, 1882-83. General Arthur St. Clair and the Ordinance of 1787, p. 13; Doyle's English Colonies in America, p. 221; McMaster's History of the United States, Vol. I, p. 271.

Vol. IV, 1883-4. The Quaker Invasion of Massachusetts, p. 32; German Mercenaries in the Revolutionary War, p. 305.

Vol. V, 1884-85. Discoveries of America; The Lost Atlantic Theory, p. 97; Thomas Hutchinson, p. 54; Arnold's Life of Abraham Lincoln, p. 261; The Pocahontas Story, p. 318.

Vol. VI, 1885-86. Hosmer's Samuel Adams, p. 65; McMaster's History of the United States, Vol. II, p. 110; Winsor's Narrative and Critical History of America, p. 317.

Vol.

The Dial, Chicago, Continued.
Vol. VII, 1886-87. Thomas Hutchinson, p. 102; Preston's Documents Illustrative of American History, p. 155; Adam's Emancipation of Massachusetts, p. 263.
Vol. VIII, 1887-88. The Sessions of the Western Lands, p. 285; Winsor's Narrative and Critical History of America, p. 337.
Vol. IX, 1888-89. Winsor's Narrative and Critical History of America, p. 127; Hosmer's Sir Henry Vane, p. 317.
Vol. XI, 1890-91. The Persistence of Historic Myths, p. 43; Economic and Social History of New England, p. 279.
Vol. XII, 1891-92. John Dickinson, p. 71; Winsor's Christopher Columbus, p. 421.
Vol. XIII. 1892. Patrick Henry, p. 41.

NEWSPAPERS.

Chicago Tribune:
J. E. Cook's History of Virginia. Sept. 22, 1883.
Geo. Bancroft's Tenth Volume of History of the United States, December 18, 1874. (Reprinted Boston Transcript, July 1, 1875.)
Yale in 1700, Jan. 10. 1875.

Palfrey's

34 William Frederick Poole.

Chicago Tribune, Continued.
Palfrey's New England, 4th vol., March 25, 1876.
Sam Peters and His Blue Laws, Dec. 22, 1877.
Samuel Sewell's Diary, Nov. 8, 1879.
Fraudulent Mather Letter on "Bagging Penn," May 23, 1870; June 11, 1870; Aug. 10, 1878; Aug. 17, 1878; Dec. 9, 1878.
Chicago Times:
Early American Books, May 12, 1876
Yale in Literature, Jan. 6, 1878.
Chicago Evening Post:
Fraudulent Mather Letter, May 26, 1891; Jan. 13, 1892.
Chicago Evening Journal:
Rutherford B. Hayes, June 17, 1876.
Bayard Family, July 8, 1880.
Salem Register:
Nathaniel Mather, Sept. 12, 1870.

———

Note.—For a condensed history of Dr. Poole, see the sketch of him in Appleton's New Cyclopedia of American History, by Mr. Daniel Goodwin.